"First the nightshirt.
Then the cap," he mumbles.

"Glass of warm milk.
Good for relaxing."

"Brush my teeth,
up and down!"

"Tuck in Guinea Pig Gus."

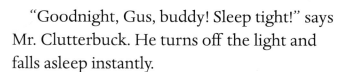

"Set the alarm, and hit the hay!"

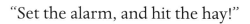

"Goodnight, Gus, buddy! Sleep tight!" says
Mr. Clutterbuck. He turns off the light and
falls asleep instantly.
  "Goodnight, Clutterbuck," answers Gus.

But what's this? Mr. Clutterbuck bolts upright in bed. Sound asleep, he trots out into the street. Mr. Clutterbuck is the town's busiest sleepwalker, although he himself doesn't know it.

"Bzzz PSHAW . . . ha ha . . . Bzzz PSHAW!" snores Mr. Clutterbuck. He must be having a good dream.

"Here we go again," sighs Gus. "Running after a sleepwalker is a job in itself!"

MAURI KUNNAS
TARJA KUNNAS

GOODNIGHT MR. CLUTTERBUCK

TRANSLATED FROM THE FINNISH BY JILL G. TIMBERS

"Look, Emmy! Our neighbor's on the move again," says Pekka. "Should we wake him up?"

"Never wake a sleepwalker," Emmy replies. "He could get a terrible shock or have some kind of fit, who knows!"

elsewhere
editions

"Rollery bowlery bzzz-pshaw!" Mr. Clutterbuck snores, marching straight into the supermarket parking lot.

"What are you doing?" Gus cries as his master hops into an empty shopping cart.

"Bowlery rollery bvroom pshaw," Mr. Clutterbuck brays.

"Stop!" Gus squeals.

"Wow, what a speed devil!" a young couple calls out.

Mr. Clutterbuck flies past in his cart like an experienced skater.

Meanwhile, in the center of town things are heating up. Two rival motorcycle gangs, the Gas Hoppers and the Boltnuts, are on the warpath again.

"My bike'll wipe out that old heap of junk any day," shouts Roar, leader of the Gas Hoppers. "What'd you do, borrow your grandma's spinning wheel?"

"You're one to talk, on that kicksled!" bellows Rip, leader of the Boltnuts. "I'll race you!"

"You punks! Let people sleep in peace!" an old lady yells from a window.

But Rip and Roar don't hear a thing, their motorcycles are making such a racket.

Mr. Clutterbuck whizzes toward the center of town.

"Brake!" Gus pleads.

Suddenly the street makes a sharp turn and the shopping cart is zipping across the yard of the laundromat.

"Bum biddly bum!" says Mr. Clutterbuck, bouncing back onto the street with the clothesline caught on his horn.

Oh, no! At that very moment Rip and Roar are gunning it full force down the main street! Vrrrroooom…

CRASH!!!

Everyone pulls through in one piece, but what a mess! Motorcycle parts and pieces and nuts and bolts, along with the bikers themselves, are strewn all over the street in a tangle of freshly washed laundry.

"Check out Roar! He looks like a reindeer!" Rip shouts.

"You should see yourself!" Roar chortles. "Bring me a mirror! Ha ha ha!"

The Gas Hoppers and the Boltnuts are screaming with laughter so loudly that they wake Mrs. Drum, who owns the laundromat.

"My clean laundry!" she thunders. "Into the laundromat, you hooligans! You can wash every single piece of clothing all over again!"

"Chug, chug, chug," murmurs Mr. Clutterbuck as he trundles homeward, an exhausted little Gus at his heels.

The next morning Mr. Clutterbuck wakes up bright and cheery. "Gus is sure out like a light," he notes. He fetches the newspaper.

Some peculiar contraption is hanging on the coat rack in the hall.

"How'd that get there?" Mr. Clutterbuck wonders.

The morning news reports that Baroness von Gurgle's valuable collection of christening spoons has disappeared and that the biker gangs have made peace during the night.

"Can't fight when we can't stop laughing!" Rip cackles on the TV screen. "Besides, we're working our tails off in Mrs. Drum's laundromat."

"Working your tails off! Baloney!" sputters Mrs. Drum. "Every time I turn my back, Roar tugs a pair of underpants onto his head and they all split their seams laughing."

In the office that day, Mr. Clutterbuck keeps rocking and spinning in his chair.

"What's up with Clutterbuck today?" his colleagues wonder.

After work, Mr. Clutterbuck bumps into his neighbor Mr. Gekkovich at the store.

"I bought some ham hocks and sausage," Mr. Gekkovich says. "I thought I'd have a cookout. Come eat with us!"

"Thank you, but I never eat much before bed," Mr. Clutterbuck replies. "Sensitive stomach."

In the evening, good smells waft from his neighbor's grill over to Mr. Clutterbuck's nose.

"We'll just munch on some carrots," Mr. Clutterbuck tells Gus. "Much healthier!"

As soon as the lights are out, Mr. Clutterbuck is off again.

"Diggety doggety hot dog!" he mutters as he bumps into Mr. Gekkovich's grill.

The grill tongs catch on Mr. Clutterbuck's horn. This draws a crowd immediately! "Yummy! Here's a guy to follow!" the town's dogs bark gleefully.

LARDY LINKS

WALLY'S WIENIES

COFFEEWURST

On the other side of town, Wally Wurst who owns the sausage factory is still in his office. "No one wants my sausages! My factory's going bankrupt," he sobs.

INVOICE

BILL

Wally Wurst is wailing so woefully that he doesn't notice the peculiar crowd bursting into his sausage factory. He hasn't bothered to lock the factory for ages, because not even burglars want his sausages.

Wally is just about to drag himself home when he hears loud chomping noises on the other side of the wall.

"Who's there?" he shouts. He peeks into the warehouse.

"Waiter!" Mr. Clutterbuck summons him. "Proo prah bratwurst! Cutlets, please!"

Wally Wurst is outraged. "This is all I need! Out of here, every last one of you!"

"Hee hee! Mama's sausage soup!" Mr. Clutterbuck giggles.

The dogs howl and scratch at the door, trying furiously to get back inside.

Wally Wurst is astonished. Then it hits him.

"Wait a minute... The mutts are nuts for my sausages! What if..."

The next morning, Mr. Clutterbuck is puzzled. His stomach's about to burst and he doesn't even want breakfast.

"Was that – BURP – second carrot too much?" he groans.

The morning news reports that Wally Wurst's factory will now be fully dedicated to producing dog food. All the dogs in town have gathered at the warehouse door, where the delighted owner is distributing samples to the test group.

"They're howling with joy!" Wally beams. "Why didn't I think of this sooner?"

"All the porridge spoons have disappeared from the military base," the news anchor continues, but Gus isn't interested in that. He has stuffed himself with hot dogs and now he needs to sleep.

Mr. Clutterbuck rides home from work with his friends. They're in splendid spirits, bellowing out the latest hits together.

"We're going to karaoke tonight," his friends tell him. "Come with us!"

"I can't sing," Mr. Clutterbuck blushes. "I should just turn in early."

But that evening in the shower when he's sure no one can hear, Mr. Clutterbuck musters his courage, clears his throat and begins to sing.

He gets so enthusiastic that he even warbles a lullabye to Gus. "Rock-a-bye, Gussy, on the tree top…" he trills.

"Ooo-ohh, saayy can you seeee," Mr. Clutterbuck belts out as he marches once again into the night, eyes closed tight. Then he switches to a marching tune. "This old man…"

An ear-splitting noise cracks in the distance, and of course Mr. Clutterbuck heads right for it.

"Halt! About face! Dangerous beasts ahead!" Gus tries to stop him.

But the racket is coming from a recording studio where the famous rock band The Runs is producing a new record.

A crowd of excited fans is camped outside the studio.

"Hey, Horn! Where do you think you're going?"

"Rocka-doodle-doo-doo, baby," Mr. Clutterbuck explains, stepping purposefully forward.

The band is hitting a wall.

"Dude, this is too tame! We need something new, something bad!" cries Ramp Fibian, the manager. "This record has to be done by morning! Can't you ramp up that chain saw?"

Just then Mr. Clutterbuck appears.

"What the . . . Who the . . . ?" Ramp's jaw drops.

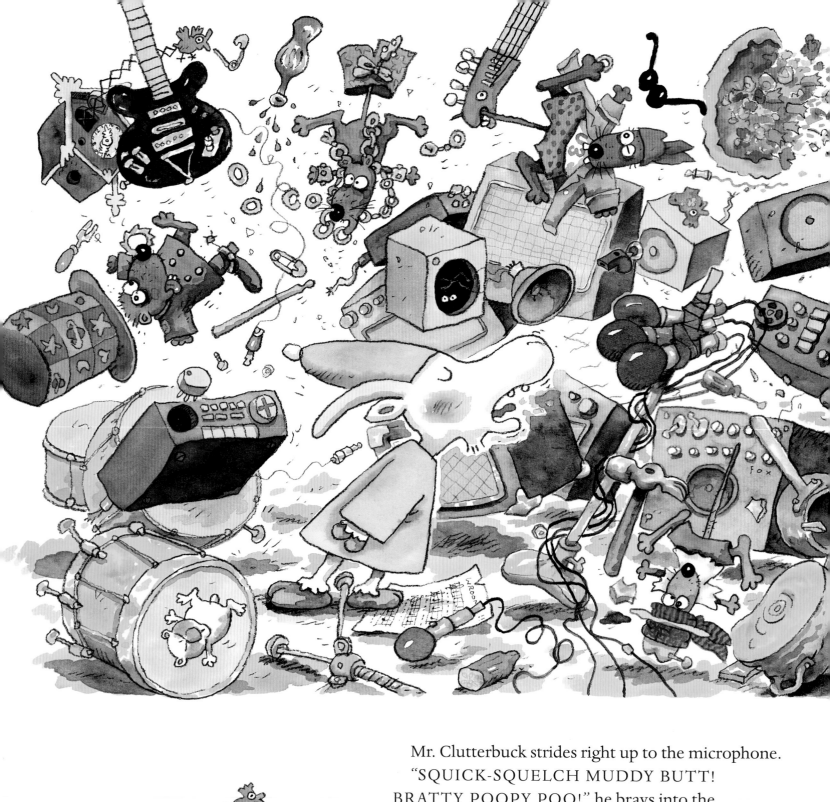

Mr. Clutterbuck strides right up to the microphone. "SQUICK-SQUELCH MUDDY BUTT! BRATTY POOPY POO!" he brays into the microphone. His bleats ring out a thousand times louder through the loudspeakers.

"That's it! You nailed it! Rude and crude and just what we need!" Ramp squeals with excitement. "Did we get it all on tape?"

The whole band is jumping up and down around Mr. Clutterbuck. "This record will top the charts! Number one! Mind-blowing, man! Join our band!"

"Nicky nacky paddywhacky and I don't give a bone!" replies Mr. Clutterbuck, stepping out the door.

"Wait! You're our new star!" Ramp shouts. "You can't leave now!"

"New star?" the groupies cry. "Autograph! Wait!"

"This old man came racing home," pants Mr. Clutterbuck.

"Did I have a nightmare?" Mr. Clutterbuck wonders next morning. His pajamas are in shreds and his ears are ringing.

"Or is this one of your pranks, Gus, you rascal?"

Gus is totally zonked. He doesn't answer.

The news reports that the Prime Minister's cod liver oil spoon has been stolen and that The Runs have released a new record.

"We've got a hit! The new lead singer is a find!" raves Manager Ramp Fibian. "Although he did, um, slip away from us..."

The Runs' new song is playing everywhere.

"Very odd," Mr. Clutterbuck mutters. "My ears are still ringing."

That evening the movie *Hot Moves* is on TV.

"I wonder if I can dance?" Mr. Clutterbuck muses. He takes a few tentative dance steps.

But soon he's exhausted and drifts off to sleep.

"What are you up to now?" Gus cries when Mr. Clutterbuck bolts up, goes into the washroom and hangs the washing machine drainpipe around his neck.

"Tux and tails and hit the rails," Mr. Clutterbuck prattles, heading outside.

"Who are you calling at this hour? It's the middle of the night!" Gus exclaims.

"Foxtrot rumba samba zumba! Tracks and swing yeah that's the thing!" Mr. Clutterbuck babbles into the phone.

A minute later, Mr. Clutterbuck has a companion.

"Doe C. Doe! Another sleepwalker!" little Gus wails.

"Tango hula bluegrass twist!" Mr. Clutterbuck chants.

"Cha cha cha," replies Doe.

The couple high-step it straight to the railroad station.

"Not onto the tracks!" shrieks Gus.

"Sure thing, tracks and swing!" Mr. Clutterbuck says. "Señorita, por favor!"

Mucker Mack, messiest mess maker in town, is also at the station.

"Look, pals! Weirdos!" says Rob's chum Squab.

"They don't see us. Just keep on mucking!" snaps Mucker Mack.

"Twist and flail and leap the rail!" Doe shouts, slapping her backside.

Squab gapes. "They must be having their own little do."

"Now they're doing the chicken dance!"

"They're rocking out!" "Mish mash mosh!" giggles Doe.

Suddenly the mess maker catches on. "I'd say those too aren't even awake!" Mucker Mack declares.

"You're right. They're sound asleep even though they're dancing," Squab agrees.

But the sweaty swingers have worked up a thirst.

"Just stay quiet so they don't wake up," Mack whispers.

Huffing and puffing, Mr. Clutterbuck steps over to the tank car and grasps the faucet.

extra strong MUSTARD

"Bunny hop!" Squab laughs.
"Forward, backwards, hop, hop, hop!"
Mr. Clutterbuck calls.

"I can't take it!" Squab guffaws.
"Wiggle jiggle wham bam!" the dancers warble.

"Stop! Stop! That's not soda pop!"
shrieks Gus.
GLOOBLE BLOOBLE SPLASH!
At least five hundred barrels of extra
spicy mustard shoot out of the pipe and
onto the railroad yard.

"Glub glub," burbles Mack.
"Musta Busta Turdy Gurdy,"
snores Mr. Clutterbuck,
escorting his lady away.

25

The next morning Mr. Clutterbuck is perplexed again. Someone has tracked mustard all over the room and even smeared him with it! And the washing machine drainpipe is hanging from his neck! "This is certainly strange! Who made such a mess?" Mr. Clutterbuck marvels.

The news reports that Mucker Mack's band of mess makers has been captured.

"Some loony dancers made that mess!" Mack protests, but no one believes him.

The spoon thief has swiped a box of shiny shoehorns from Mr. Slipper's shoe store.

"Must have thought they were soup spoons. Where can the thief be hiding all these spoons?" Mr. Clutterbuck ponders.

During the day Mr. Clutterbuck behaves very strangely.
"You stick your tongue out, you fold your ankles in," he sings to himself.

In the evening Mr. Clutterbuck hears the neighbor and his children returning from the amusement park.
"The roller coaster was great!" the children shriek.
"The Liquidizer was better!"
"The Turbo Whip was the best of all!"

"Good thing I don't have to go on those rides," Mr. Clutterbuck says as he washes the mustard from his pajamas. "Even just watching the spin cycle makes me dizzy."

Soon Mr. Clutterbuck's snores again echo over the empty streets.
"Where are we going tonight?" Gus wonders. "Sporting a real party hat, to boot."

27

He should have guessed. Mr. Clutterbuck is of
course aiming right for the amusement park.
He rides the roller coaster first.
"Yippee ai ee!" Mr. Clutterbuck bellows.
"Eeek!" squeals Gus.

Next Mr. Clutterbuck tries the Cyclone,

and then the Gut Churner,

the Shake'n'Quake,

and last, the Turbo Whip.

"Upsy down and round and round and high and low we go!" carols Mr. Clutterbuck.
"Dumdy dum," replies Gus.

TOMMY
THE TALKING BULL

DO NOT DISTURB

Mr. Clutterbuck totters over to the park's top draw, Tommy the Talking Bull. He goes right into the bull's enclosure.

"Good day, hello there, Mr. President," Mr. Clutterbuck intones.

"Hunh?" says the sleepy bull.

Bulls get angry if you interrupt their sleep. Especially if you are wearing a bright red hat.

Recovering from his surprise, Tommy charges at Mr. Clutterbuck. Luckily, Mr. Clutterbuck makes a sharp turn just as the bull is about to reach him.

BOOM!

The bull slams into the tree so hard that a bird's nest falls down, right onto Mr. Clutterbuck's head. The nest is full to the brim with spoons! A furious magpie dives at Mr. Clutterbuck. "My priceless home! Nest and spoons back into the tree imMEEEDiately!" the bird screams.

"Tweety sweetie purty birdie," replies Mr. Clutterbuck cheerfully. He weaves his way over to the police station.

"What's going on here?" asks Constable Fuzz. "Look at this! All the town's lost spoons! And Picklock Pete, the thief with the longest grab in the region!"

"We're not all born with a silver spoon in our mouth!" the magpie shrills.

The television news crew is on the spot in an instant, and this time Mr. Clutterbuck, hero of the night, makes it onto the news.

"The town has this quick-witted passerby to thank! Would you please tell our viewers how you located Picklock Pete's stash?" the interviewer inquires politely.

"Dizzle Whizzle Sizzle SPOON!" explains Mr. Clutterbuck. He bows, and exits the scene.

"Umm, yes. Of course," stammers the interviewer.

Next morning, Mr. Clutterbuck wakes up feeling bright and cheery. But he jumps when he looks in the mirror.

Just then he hears shouting outside: "GOOD MORNING, MR. CLUTTERBUCK!"

A whole crowd of townsfolk are standing in his yard.

"We've done some investigating and ascertained just who's been improving things around here lately," Constable Fuzz declares. "We found out who's behind the fact that the motorcycle gangs made peace, Wally Wurst's sausage factory was saved from bankruptcy, the Runs had a gold record, Mucker Mack

opened a cleaning company and the townspeople can once again use their own spoons for their soups and puddings!"

Mayor Ellie Gance and the whole town council are present.

"On behalf of the whole town we wish to present you with a token of our appreciation, Mr. Clutterbuck."

"But...but...I didn't..." stammers Mr. Clutterbuck. "Is this a joke?"

Mr. Clutterbuck received a fine gift, indeed: an electric treadmill.
Even Gus couldn't have come up with a better present.

The next evening, Mr. Clutterbuck is hoofing it again.
"Goodnight, Mr. Clutterbuck! Enjoy yourself," sighs Gus, happily
pulling the blanket up to his ears.
All is well…just as long as the power doesn't go out.